JAMES

PERCY

MEET ALL THESE FRIENDS IN BUZZ BOOKS:

The Animals of Farthing Wood
Thomas the Tank Engine
James Bond Junior
Fireman Sam
Joshua Jones
Blinky Bill
Rupert
Babar

First published 1990 by Buzz Books
an imprint of Reed Children's Books
Michelin House, 81 Fulham Rd, London SW3 6RB
and Auckland, Melbourne, Singapore and Toronto
Reprinted 1993
Copyright © William Heineman Ltd 1990
All publishing rights: William Heinemann Ltd
All television and merchandising rights licensed by
William Heinemann Ltd to Britt Allcroft (Thomas) Ltd
exclusively, worldwide
Photographs © Britt Allcroft (Thomas) Ltd 1985, 1986
Photographs by David Mitton, Kenny McArthur and
Terry Permane for Britt Allcroft's production of
Thomas the Tank Engine and Friends
ISBN 1 85591 027 6
Printed and bound in Italy by Olivotto

THOMAS AND BERTIE

buzz books

One day Thomas was waiting at a
junction when a bus came into the yard.

"Hullo!" said Thomas. "Who are you?"

"I'm Bertie," said the bus. "Who are
you?"

"I'm Thomas. I run this branch line."

Bertie laughed. "Ah – I remember now!" he said. "You were stuck in the snow. I had to take your passengers, then Terence the tractor had to pull you out! I've come to help you with your passengers today."

"Help *me*?" said Thomas, crossly. "I can go faster than you," he said, going bluer than ever and letting off steam.

"You can't," said Bertie.

"I can," huffed Thomas.

"I'll race *you*!" said Bertie.

9

Their drivers agreed to the race. The
Station Master shouted, "Are you ready?
GO!" – and they were off!

It always took Thomas a little while to build up speed so Bertie quickly drew in front.

Thomas was running well but he did not hurry. "Why don't you go fast? Why don't you go fast?" called Annie and Clarabel,

who were running along behind.

"Wait and see. Wait and see," hissed
Thomas.

"He's a long way ahead, a long way
ahead," they cried, anxiously.

But Thomas didn't mind; he had remembered the level crossing.

There was Bertie fuming at the crossing gates while they sailed gaily through.

"Goodbye, Bertie!" called Thomas.

After that the road left the railway and went through a village. They couldn't see Bertie any more.

Before long they had to stop at a station to let off passengers. "Peep, pip, peep! Quickly, please," called Thomas.

Everybody got out quickly. The guard blew his whistle and off they went again.

"Come along! Come along!" sang
Thomas.

"We're coming along! We're coming
along!" said Annie and Clarabel.

Thomas looked straight ahead and whistled in horror. There was Bertie crossing the bridge over the railway, tooting triumphantly on his horn!

"Oh, deary me! Oh, deary me!" groaned Thomas.

"Steady, Thomas," said Thomas's driver. "We'll beat Bertie yet."

Annie and Clarabel joined in. "We'll beat Bertie yet! We'll beat Bertie yet!" they sang.

"We'll do it! We'll do it!" puffed Thomas, bravely. "Oh bother, there's a station."

As Thomas stopped at the station he heard Bertie, tooting loudly.

"Goodbye, Thomas! You must be tired," called Bertie, as he raced by. "Sorry I can't stop; we buses have to work you know! Goodbye."

"Oh, dear!" thought Thomas. "We've lost." But he felt better after a drink. Then the signal dropped to show that the line was clear and they were off again.

As they rumbled over the bridge they saw Bertie waiting at the traffic lights. When the lights turned green, Bertie started with a roar and chased on after Thomas again.

Road and railway ran up the valley side by side. By now Thomas had reached his full speed. Bertie tried hard but Thomas was too fast.

On and on they raced. Excited passengers cheered and shouted across the valley as Thomas whistled triumphantly and plunged into the tunnel, leaving Bertie toiling far behind.

"We've done it! We've done it!" chanted Annie and Clarabel happily, as they whooshed into the last station.

Everybody was there to give Thomas three cheers for winning the race. They all gave Bertie a big welcome too.

"Well done, Thomas!" said Bertie. "That was fun. But to beat you over that hill I should have had to grow wings and be an aeroplane!"

Now Thomas and Bertie keep each other very busy. Bertie finds people in the villages who want to go by train and takes them to Thomas, while Thomas brings people to the station for Bertie to take home.

Bertie and Thomas often talk about their race. But Bertie's passengers don't like being bounced like peas in a frying pan!

The Fat Controller has warned Thomas not to race at dangerous speeds. So although Thomas and Bertie would like to have another race, I don't think they ever will. Do you?

THOMAS

EDWARD

GORDON